Back To Passion

Collection Of Poems

By

S. Y. Pompey

Back To Passion
Copyright © 2024 by S. Y. Pompey

All rights reserved. No part of this publication may be reproduced, distributed, or transmitted in any form or by any means, including photocopying, recording, or other electronic or mechanical methods, without the prior written permission of the author, except in the case of brief quotations embodied in critical reviews and certain other non-commercial uses permitted by copyright law.

Tellwell Talent
www.tellwell.ca

ISBN
978-1-77962-220-4 (Paperback)
978-1-77962-221-1 (eBook)

Table of Contents

Acknowledgement vii
If I Should Have You 3
Our Connection 5
Mysterious Ways 7
A Stroll 9
With Your Eyes 11
Your Innocence 13
Come to See Me 15
Show Me Your Heart 17
The Country 19
Your Scent 21
Thinking of You 23
I Go To Pieces 25
Your White Shirt 27
In Bed 29
Late For Work 31
You Were Singing 33
Into The Woods 35
Down By The River 37
Missing You 39
Dreaming of You 41

This book is written for those who seek passion.

S.Y. Pompey

Acknowledgement

Very special thanks to both Andre Ostrovsky for all of his work and support; and to Victor Ostrovsky for editing.

Thanks to Niall O'Sullivan and Zachary Cunningham for my beautiful creative space.

Dedicated to The Dane

--

SYP

Back To Passion

S. Y. POMPEY

If I Should Have You

If I should have you
For a minute, a day or two
If I should have you
For a week, a month or two
If I should have you cause
I'm attracted to you
If I should have you cause
I know you're attracted to me too
If I can't have a moment
A minute, or a day or two with you
Then I'd always wonder what it
Would have been like to be with you

S. Y. Pompey

Our Connection

Your elegant ways
Soft smile
Your soft hair covers your brows
Mystery
Your strong strides
A glance
The game for months and days
I waited
There you are
Regal, beautiful
The connection

Mysterious Ways

A look, a stare
A game, many games
You spoke, one sentence
A surprise
You touched me, I froze
I can't breathe

S. Y. Pompey

A Stroll

We strolled along many streets
We talked, laughed
Through the paths we sauntered
Stories told, hand in hand
Along the streets we strolled
Flower you picked
The flower you then tucked behind my ear

With Your Eyes

With your eyes you spoke to me
Come
I want to be close to you
Come closer
Look at me, talk to me
Softly
I want to get to know you
Look at me

Your Innocence

The innocence in your touch
It is in your smile, you blush
The innocence in your eyes
I'll take care of your heart

S. Y. Pompey

Come to See Me

You are coming soon
To see me, to be with me
You are coming to see me
My heart beating fast
Racing, fluttering
You are here

Show Me Your Heart

Show me your heart
I'll be gentle
With every stroke
I'll cradle it
Keeping it close to me
I'll guard it
From pain and hurt
I'll protect it
Show me your heart
And show you mine

The Country

Come with me to the country
We will walk hand in hand
We will dine
Come with me to the country
You can chase me through the meadow
Seduce me
Come with me to the country
You'll lie on top of me
You'll kiss me deep, in the high grass

Your Scent

Your scent draws me near
Intense
A whiff makes my heart race
Turbulence
Your scent is intoxicating
Lightheaded

Thinking of You

As I lay here
I think about sitting on your thighs
I feel the pressure of your squeeze
I squeeze back
Your body pressing, we're meshing
I forgot to breathe, I find air
Eyes searching
Learning, wanting
Heart races, words lost
World forgotten
Movements slow
Eyes closed

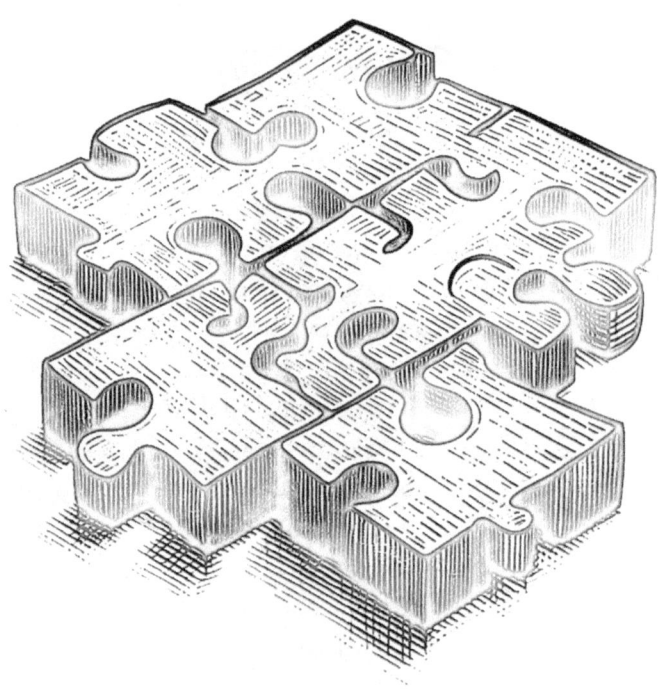

I Go To Pieces

You call me baby
I just go to pieces

Your White Shirt

You walk in wearing a white shirt
I stare, in awe
Untucked, I gazed
I touched your chest
You walk in wearing a white shirt
Your slow walk, smooth
You approach me
I couldn't speak

In Bed

Naked
I kiss your nose
Free
I kiss your neck
Laughing
I nibble your belly
Smiling
I bit your lips
With tears
I said I love you

S. Y. Pompey

Late For Work

I was late for work
Cause you held me tight
I was late for work
Because I didn't want you out of my sight

S. Y. Pompey

You Were Singing

I heard you sing this morning
Low, sweet
To me
You were singing this morning
I heard you sing this morning
Happy, fun
I heard you singing
I heard you sing this morning
For me from you
You were singing this morning

Into The Woods

You walked with me into the woods
Twigs cracked under our feet
You walked with me into the woods
Birds chirped
They darted between the trees
You walked with me into the woods
You handed me a wild flower
I placed it between your lips

S. Y. Pompey

Down By The River

I stared at your reflection
As it gently danced
Into the clear water
I gazed at your reflection
The sun a halo above your head
I touched the water
You kicked at the water
With your bare feet
It drenched my back

Missing You

Missing the one who tickles me
Everyday
Missing the one who massages me
Everywhere
Into deep relaxation
No nightmares
Missing the one whom I kiss
Everyday
Because you left and went to another
Hemisphere

Dreaming of You

You are next to me
In bed
Caressing my face
I'm nibbling your ear
Pulling you closer
Ooh I'm awake

www.ingramcontent.com/pod-product-compliance
Lightning Source LLC
LaVergne TN
LVHW042004060526
838200LV00041B/1862